# LITTLE

# LiON

# RESCUE

STRIPES PUBLISHING LTD
An imprint of the Little Tiger Group
1 Coda Studios, 189 Munster Road, London SW6 6AW

A paperback original
First published in Great Britain in 2019

Text copyright © Rachel Delahaye, 2019
Inside illustrations copyright © Artful Doodlers, 2019
Cover illustration copyright © Suzie Mason, 2019

ISBN: 978-1-78895-068-8

The right of Rachel Delahaye, and Suzie Mason and
Artful Doodlers to be identified as the author and illustrators of
this work respectively has been asserted by them in accordance
with the Copyright, Designs and Patents Act, 1988.

A CIP catalogue record for this book is available from the British Library.

# LITTLE
# LiON
# RESCUE

## Rachel Delahaye

This is dedicated to my grandmother, Rosemary,
who loved animals and fought for their rights
– Rachel

# CONTENTS

## The Big Clean-Up

"Oh, yuck! You're covered in elephant dung!" Ella held her nose and pointed at Fliss's overalls.

"You can't muck out elephants without getting a little bit dirty." Fliss grinned. "If you're clean, it means you didn't work hard enough!"

"I'd rather be lazy than stinky," Ella said, flicking mud and straw from her fingers.

Jonty, the zookeeper, clapped his

hands together loudly.

"Wheelbarrows down, everyone," he called. "Gather round."

The girls joined the rest of their school group at the gate, where Jonty laughed at the state of them.

"So how was that? Smelly?"

Everyone made *poowee* noises and giggled.

"Elephants eat for up to sixteen hours a day, which means they produce a lot of … muck. If you look behind you, you'll see the elephants waiting to come back into the enclosure."

The giant grey beasts were behind the next gate, their ears flapping gently.

"I hope they say thank you to us for cleaning their house!" Ella said.

"I think they'll be very pleased," Jonty said. "Can you see how their tails are swishing from side to side? It means they're happy."

"How do we know when they're *not* happy?" Fliss asked. She wished she had brought a book to take notes.

"I've been lucky enough to spend time with these animals in the wild," Jonty said. "I've seen them in all sorts of moods. If their tails go stiff or they spread their ears out wide, then they may be nervous. If they make a trumpeting sound, then get out of there fast! It could mean they're about to charge."

Fliss closed her eyes and imagined it – a happy herd of elephants suddenly startled, ears wide and trunks raised, trumpeting their alarm… Jonty clapped his hands again and she opened her eyes, hoping no one had seen her daydreaming.

"Right, these beauties need to come in and cool off in the water. You lot could do with some cooling off, too! Your teacher says there's ice cream waiting for you in the school centre, just as soon as you get out of those overalls. Off to the wash room!"

There was a big cheer as the children hurried out of the enclosure, shouting "Ice cream, ice cream!". Fliss was the last to go. She would stay forever if she could, even if it *was* smelly.

She tugged the zookeeper's sleeve. "My name is Fliss. Can I ask you something?"

"Of course." Over her head, he beckoned to the other zookeepers, who began to lead the herd back into the enclosure. Fliss watched them in wonder – how did these large animals move so gracefully?

"Fliss, did you have a question?"

"Yes. Sorry!" Fliss blushed. "I just wanted to know how you became a zookeeper."

"Well, I knew what I wanted to do from a very young age. I learned all I could about animals and when I was old enough I volunteered at rescue centres all over Africa. It took a lot of patience and passion but now I'm here, in charge of elephants and lions. It's my perfect job."

"You're so lucky being with animals all day long."

"Is this what you want to do when you grow up?"

"I want to be a vet," Fliss said. "I want to help animals who are in trouble."

"Being a vet is a tough job!" Jonty

said. "But it looks to me like you have determination. That's a great start."

"Jonty?" Fliss said, thinking of something. "If you're in charge of the lions, does that mean you can tell them to wake up?" She had been so excited for the zoo trip but with a particular longing to see those proud creatures up close. The empty enclosure had left her feeling disappointed.

Jonty laughed. "It's not that simple, I'm afraid. I'm sorry your group didn't get to see them but if they wake before you go, I'll come and get you, OK?"

In the distance, Fliss could hear her friends calling. She wasn't interested in ice cream. She just wanted to talk to Jonty about animals.

"You'd better go," Jonty said, steering her towards the school centre. "The elephants are coming and you're not a professional animal handler – not yet, anyway."

After changing out of her overalls, Fliss found Ella in the school centre, covered in splodges of pink-and-white gunk.

"So, you don't mind getting dirty *sometimes*," Fliss said.

"No!" Ella licked the sticky liquid dripping down her wrist. "I don't mind getting messy when it's with ice cream. Are you going to have one?"

"I'm too excited to eat!" Fliss unfolded her map of the zoo and pointed to an area called Pride of Place – the lion enclosure. "The zookeeper said he'd come and get us as soon as they wake up. Isn't that great?"

"*If* they wake up, Flissy. Come on, it's the butterfly house next."

"You'd better wash your hands, then. Butterflies *love* sugar! They'll lick you all over with their long curly tongues."

Ella shrieked and ran to the wash room and Fliss smiled.

The butterfly house was going to be fun, especially now Ella was in a flap! But as they walked through the rubber doors and into the steamy room full of colourful fluttering wings, she hoped that Jonty would soon interrupt with the news that the lions had woken up.

# Free to Roam

"Urgh, it was so sticky and hot in there," Ella gasped, flapping her hands in front of her face.

"It's because the exotic butterflies need a tropical temperature," said Fliss. "I loved the big blue ones, didn't you?"

"No! All I could think about were those tongues!" Ella wrinkled her nose. "I watched one drinking... Fliss, the tongue actually *rolled* out! Butterflies are monsters!"

The teachers did a headcount of all the children, most of whom were looking soggy after their butterfly encounter. Mr Pincent was looking particularly hot and frazzled but it wasn't because of the butterfly house. Apparently, Ollie, Dan and Sarah had crept off to have another look at the crocodiles without permission and were now completely lost!

"Mrs Mullins and I are going to look for some lost pupils. The rest of you may take a last walk around the zoo," Mr Pincent said, dabbing at his face with a handkerchief. "Stay in pairs and meet back at the gift shop in fifteen minutes."

"Anyone who is late will sit at the front of the coach on the way back, next to me," Mrs Mullins added sternly.

Before she'd even finished speaking, Fliss had grabbed Ella's hand and was pulling her along the walkway.

"Whoa there, Flissy! What's the rush?"

"We've only got fifteen minutes and there's so much to see! Come on, this way."

"You're dragging me to the lions, aren't you?" Ella said, jogging to keep up. "I bet that's where we're going."

"Yup!" Fliss grinned. "I've got a feeling I'm going to meet one today."

All around them, the zoo rang with the cheeps and hoots of birds and animals, but Pride of Place was disappointingly quiet. Fliss read everything on the information boards

– about the Serengeti, the lions' native home, and about diet and behaviour and bringing up cubs. Then she paced around the enclosure fence, hoping to spot one hiding in the bushes or sleeping up on a rock.

"They're not here," Ella said impatiently. "If we wait any longer there won't be time to see anything else."

It was true. The zoo had more animal species than Fliss could name. She wasn't even sure *why* she was so desperate to see the lions.

There would be other visits to the zoo.

"Ella, you're right," Fliss said.
"Where shall we go next?"

"Let's go-go to the flamingos!" Ella
sang, wiggling her hips. "This way."

It was impossible to be sad when Ella
was around and Fliss joined in with her
friend's made-up song. They sang
*Everybody sing-o, we're going to the flamingos!*
at the tops of their voices and the other
visitors looked at them as if they were
crazy, which only made Ella sing louder.

At the flamingo pond, Ella tried to
stand on one leg for as long as possible
while Fliss read out facts from the
information board.

"Did you know that the feathers under
flamingos' wings are black and can only
been seen when they are flying? And

their pink feathers are only pink because they eat pink shrimp!"

"I thought it was for camouflage," Ella pondered.

"Only if they were hiding in a strawberry field," Fliss snorted. "And I don't think there are many of those in Africa!"

Laughing, the girls ran back to the gift shop, discussing what colour flamingos would be if they ate blueberries or chocolate or multicoloured Unicorn Pops.

At the gift shop Ollie, Dan and Sarah were standing behind Mrs Mullins, looking sheepish. Mr Pincent had gone to freshen up – which meant he was having a cup of tea to calm his nerves – so the children were allowed a few minutes to look around the shop and spend their pocket money.

"The gift shop – my favourite enclosure!" Ella cheered.

Fliss smiled but for her this was the worst part of the zoo. It meant her time with the real animals had come to an end.

"Come on. First to find a fluffy flamingo gets a … a fluffy flamingo, I guess!" Ella whooped and disappeared into the cuddly toy section, along with most of the class. Within seconds they were all play-acting with squidgy crocodiles, plush sharks and stretchy octopuses.

Fliss wasn't keen on gift-shop toys. For a start, they didn't look that realistic. The sharks' teeth were made of bendy felt, the snakes were *furry* and the cuddly flamingos did *not* have black feathers under their wings…

Instead, she was drawn to the
postcards, which were photographs of
real animals. She wanted to find one of
a butterfly drinking nectar for Ella. Just

the thought of it made her giggle. If she saw a penguin she'd get that for her mum – it was her favourite animal – and an elephant for her dad.

But what about a souvenir for herself? It was so hard to choose. From the anaconda snake that made her classmates scream to the foxy-faced zorro, Fliss loved all the animals from A to Z. She couldn't pick a favourite if she tried! Maybe a postcard of the one animal she'd missed on the day's outing would be a good choice. It wouldn't be a souvenir, more of a missing piece. Yes, she would buy herself a postcard of the lions.

# A Particular Postcard

There weren't many lion postcards – a
couple taken in the zoo and a few taken in
the wild. These ones didn't show lions as
"kings of the jungle" like picture books
did, but as kings of the African plains,
which were wide, open grasslands that
seemed to go on forever. Fliss was about
to pick one when some other cards
further along the wall caught her eye.
They were large, shiny and colourful.

When she got close she saw they

were 3D hologram pictures making the animals look like they were alive, and the pictures moved around or changed completely if you tilted them. There were great white sharks swimming then attacking, grizzly bears sitting and then standing tall, and lions, too! There was only one left and Fliss snatched it quickly, as if it might disappear.

She looked down at the picture and gasped at how lifelike it was – it was as if she were holding the lions in the very palm of her hand!

The pride was sitting in the shade of a
tree and all of them were snoozing in the
midday sun. All but one. A lioness was
standing up, her head turned to the side.
It was as if she was looking for something.
Fliss tilted the card backwards. The
picture of the pride faded away and in its
place was a single lion
cub, standing all alone,
its eyes wide with
fear. Something was
wrong. This lion
cub was lost.

Fliss bought the card
right away. There was no
way she could leave this little
cub behind, even if it *was* just a
picture! She'd give it a home on her
bedroom wall and on the coach journey

back she could pass the time making up a story with a happy ending for the lost cub. Perhaps Ella could help with a song. At that very moment Ella came up behind her, placed a long, cuddly snake on her shoulder and hissed. Fliss jumped back in surprise but when she saw what it was, she grabbed the snake and cuddled it under her chin.

"You're supposed to be scared!" Ella groaned.

"Not me… I'd love to meet a real-life snake. I'd like to wear one round my neck like a scarf."

"People would call you Fliss the Hiss!" Ella laughed.

Just then Mrs Mullins boomed her full name – Felicity – across the gift shop. Fliss looked over and knew right away

that her day was about to get better,
because standing beside Mrs Mullins was
Jonty. The lions were finally awake!

Mrs Mullins announced that she would
hold the coach for anyone who wanted
to see the lions, but Fliss's classmates
were more interested in choosing toys
and sweets for the journey home. Even
Ella wasn't that interested. She had
bought the cuddly snake and was happily
annoying people with it.

"I'm sorry but we can't delay the
journey home for just one pupil," Mrs
Mullins said. Fliss looked at Ella
pleadingly and got down on one knee,
clasping her hands together.

"Only if you promise to play pranks
with me on the way home," Ella said,
holding out her second purchase – a

tube of plastic
spiders. Fliss
leaped up and
wrapped her arms
round her.

"And I can promise
to have them back in ten
minutes…" Jonty added with a smile.

Mrs Mullins caved in and the girls ran
ahead of Jonty, laughing and waving at
the monkeys on the way. When Pride of
Place came into view, Fliss sprinted and
didn't stop until she was right there, her
face against the enclosure fence.

"Where are they? Where are they?" she
cried.

Jonty put his hands on his hips
and sighed heavily. "Boab, the big
male lion was out… But it seems he's

hidden himself away again. Lions are crepuscular, which means they mainly come out at twilight and sleep through the day. Don't take it personally. Visitors are often disappointed. We have webcams dotted around the enclosure, so when you get home you might be able to see them online."

"Oh, OK," Fliss said weakly.

"Come on, Fliss," Ella said. "Race you back to the gift shop. Let's tell the others we saw nine huge lions and a million lion cubs and make them all jealous."

"But that would be a lie," Fliss said sadly.

She took her postcard from her pocket and looked at the pride, imagining them there in front of her. Then she tilted it so she could see the cub.

"Fliss!" Ella's voice was impatient but it sounded oddly quiet, as if she was a long way away. She must have already started running back. It was time to go.

Fliss raised her eyes to look at the enclosure one last time but from out of nowhere a warm cloud of dust hit her in the face. She blinked and rubbed her eyes… Even before she opened them again, she knew something strange had happened. The air felt warmer, her skin tingled as if she was standing in strong sunlight and the echoing zoo sounds were gone.

She opened her eyes and gasped. It couldn't be possible! She had to be dreaming!

In front of her, stretching to the horizon, was an expanse of dry grasses, bleached white and yellow by the sun. The landscape was bare apart from a few lonely trees and occasional lumps of rock, some as big as houses. The sky was a wide roof of palest blue.

Fliss spun round. There was no Ella or Jonty behind her, no information board or fence, no walkway back to the gift shop. This wasn't a trick of the light or a special effect designed by the zoo for a Serengeti experience...

This *was* the Serengeti!

# Welcome to the Wild

Fliss knew all about the Serengeti National Park in Tanzania. But what she didn't know is how she got there! Was Pride of Place a portal to another dimension? Was Jonty some kind of time-travelling zookeeper? Or maybe... Fliss looked down at the postcard in her hands.

"Did you bring me here?" she asked it. "And how do I get back?"

She tipped the picture backwards and

forwards to see if it would transport her back to the zoo but nothing happened. Fliss felt a flutter of panic rising in her tummy. If she didn't get back soon, Mrs Mullins would be cross and Mr Pincent would need another cup of tea, and the coach driver might lose her patience and drive off without them all! Then something caught her eye.

In front of her was a rock and behind it she was sure she saw something move. Fliss froze. *Don't be scared*, she told herself. *If it was a big animal, I'd see its horns or ears sticking out above the rock.* She decided it had to be something small, like a bird or a hare, and crept forwards to take a look.

At the same time, the creature cautiously peeked round the rock. It wasn't a hare or a bird.

Fliss knew exactly what it was.

She held her breath as it walked unsteadily out into the open on large padded paws.

"Hey, little lion," she said softly.

And it was *definitely* a lion. Fliss quickly recognized the roundness of the ears and even though its little legs had spotty markings like a leopard, she could see the strong lion-esque features through the fluffy golden coat that covered the rest of its body. There were grey flecks on its wide nose, which was dotted with rows of white whiskers.

Fliss crouched down so she wouldn't look tall and scary and held out her hand. The cub was shaking and its eyes were big and worried. Fliss had seen that expression before. She took the postcard from her pocket, tilted it back and studied it again… A cub looking lost. She stared back at the real-life cub in front of her.

"It's *you*, isn't it?" she whispered.

The cub made a noise that sounded more like a mouse's squeak than a lion's roar. Fliss didn't know whether to laugh or cry at this little creature trying to make its voice heard.

"I can't hear you very well," she said. "How about if I come a bit closer?"

She crawled slowly on hands and knees towards the cub. Frightened, it took a step back.

"I won't hurt you," Fliss said, sitting back on her heels. "I'm here to help. I want to be a vet when I grow up, which means I care a lot about animals. You probably don't understand a word I'm saying. You've probably never heard a human talk. Perhaps you've never seen a human at all! Well, now you have and I promise you I'm very friendly."

Fliss laughed at herself, talking such gibberish, and imagined what Ella would make of it. She'd say: "you're more like Doctor Do-lally than Doctor Dolittle, Flissy!" But although Fliss really did wish she could talk to animals (and *Doctor Dolittle* was her favourite story), what she said didn't need to make sense, it just needed to make the cub feel safe. And it looked as if it was working.

The cub began to take little steps fowards, its eyes fixed on her.

"That's it." Fliss reached her hand out further for the cub to sniff. "It's all going to be OK."

The cub rubbed its cheek against the back of her hand and Fliss was able to

stretch out
her fingers
and scratch
the fur behind
the cub's ear.
It closed its eyes
in bliss. When she
stopped, it shook its head from
side to side and leaped right up on to
her lap.

"Does this mean we're friends?" Fliss
laughed, stroking along the cub's back.
"Then we'd better get to know more
about each other. I'm Fliss. If you
have a name I don't suppose I could
pronounce it. I don't speak lion-ese.
I'm ten years old. How old are you, I
wonder?"

The cub wobbled in her lap and fell

off. It bounced back up again.

"Let's have a good look at you," Fliss said, confident that the cub trusted her. "You're a little bit scrawny, bigger than the average cat, but smaller than a dog. And look at those lovely wide paws! Hmmm, I'm guessing you're about three months old."

Fliss thought back to the information boards at the zoo. It said cubs didn't become independent until they were two years old.

"Alone and so young! You probably still need your mother's milk as well as fresh meat. Oh my goodness, your mother must be worried sick. How on earth did you get lost in the first place?"

Lifting the cub up into her arms, Fliss stood and looked around her. She could see herds of grey animals in the distance – buffalo, perhaps. Lions would be hard to see as their golden fur would be camouflaged by the grasses, so Fliss listened out for a sound on the wind – the territorial roar of a male lion or a mother lion calling for her baby.

"Let's be as quiet as we can," she whispered to her new friend. The lion cub mewed. "Shh, noisy one!"

Fliss turned in circles, trying to distinguish the different sounds of the Serengeti. There was the swishing of the wind as it whipped across the grasses and occasional cries of birds. But there was no roar. Fliss didn't know what to do next but she had to do *something*.

"I have to find a way home," she said. "But not until we've found your mother."

# A Suitable Name

"We're going to do some exploring,"
she said to the baby in her arms. The
cub reached up its soft paw and patted
her face. "I could cuddle you forever!"
She laughed. "But we need to get you
home. Look, there's a trail. We'll start
by going that way."

Hoping the path through the grass
was made by the footsteps of lions,
Fliss set off. After a short walk she
came to an area where the grasses had

been crushed completely flat and in some places torn up. The earth beneath was ochre-coloured and scarred with deep scratches.

The cub whined. Fliss put it down and let it sniff the ground.

"What is it, little lion? Is it a smell you know?"

While the cub turned in circles following its nose, Fliss searched the ground for clues. Then she found one, a tuft of coarse ginger hair. It must have come from a lion's mane! Had there been a fight – a clash between prides over food or territory?

In her mind, Fliss pictured the battle, all claws and jaws and sharp, sharp teeth. Frightening sounds and little cubs running for safety across the vast Serengeti, searching for a place to hide. Fliss hated to think her little cub might have been caught up in such a scary scene but it looked like a possibility.

"Yes, this could be where you got lost," Fliss said to the cub, who was still sniffing. "Come on. Your family isn't here now but we will find them, I promise you."

It was a big promise and Fliss hoped that she could keep it. It wasn't like the promises she normally made, such as playing with Ella at break time or scraping the plates after dinner. This was the Serengeti! She took a moment to

look around. The landscape was empty
and barren, and far, far away from
anything she knew.

She raised her hand to shield her eyes
from the light as she looked out for lions
or people or something that might help,
but it was impossible to see. The heat
was making the air ripple, the landscape
bend and the colours blend together. It
was hard to focus on anything.

Meanwhile, the lion cub had started running away, almost tripping up on its heavy paws.

Fliss smiled. "You want to go that way, do you?"

But the cub wasn't following a trail or a scent. It was chasing a giant grasshopper. When Fliss realized, she laughed so loudly she took herself by surprise.

"That looks fun!" She joined in the chase, running alongside the cub in pursuit of the hopper, getting close but never managing to catch it.

"This is impossible!" Fliss panted. The cub was clearly thinking the same thing because it lay down with a big thump. Its chest was rising and falling fast, and Fliss scooped up the cub in her arms.

"Weren't we silly, running around in the midday sun?" she said. She should have known better. The little lion was just a baby and babies were vulnerable. Until they found the pride, Fliss was its only chance of survival. If she really wanted to be a vet, now was the time to prove she had what it took.

"With hand on heart, I promise to care for animals in need of help and I will not rest until they are well again. That's my very own vet's oath," Fliss explained to the cub, who blinked back. "That means I won't leave you until you're safe."

Under the shade of a tree, Fliss laid the cub down and pulled off her backpack. There was a bottle of water inside it. She poured some of the water into her cupped hand and the cub began to lap it up thirstily. Its tongue was prickly like sandpaper against her palm – the same as Ella's cat, Bobkin – and Fliss shook her head in wonderment. Wasn't it incredible how house cats were so similar to these wild ones? The only difference really was size. Just think if Bobkin was the size of a lion… They would need a bigger scratching post for a start and he would bring home much larger things than mice. Looking at the cub now, it was hard to imagine that one day it would grow up to be a hunter. It looked more like a teddy bear!

When the cub finished drinking, Fliss tried to swig the last bit of water from the bottle, but the cub brushed against her arm and knocked the bottle out of her hands. The rest of the water soaked into the ground. It didn't matter – at least the lion was looking brighter, although it was still a bit wobbly on its legs. It needed food.

"Hang on," Fliss said, remembering what was in her bag. "I've got something you might like."

She had been far too excited to eat all of her lunch at the zoo. While the other kids sat along the trestle tables scoffing their sandwiches and crisps, Fliss had been reading the posters pinned on the walls – life cycles of insects, caring for baby animals, hostile environments, endangered species. In fact, she'd only nibbled half a sandwich and an apple before Mr Pincent had begun making a fuss and telling them to "get a move on". She had been annoyed but now it turned out that not finishing lunch was a blessing in disguise. She had leftover food for the cub.

Fliss unwrapped her remaining sandwich. It was chicken and salad. She guessed lions didn't eat salad, but she held out the piece of cold roast chicken and the cub took it between its teeth.

"I know you don't usually cook your meat but it's all I've got, I'm afraid."

The cub gulped it down then looked at her expectantly.

"More? I'm not sure if there is anything else…"

Fliss rummaged in her lunchbox. She didn't think an apple core would be welcome. Or her box of raisins.

"Aha!" There, wrapped in silver foil, was something that might do. "I'm sure lions would eat eggs if there was nothing else on the menu. Perhaps, if they were really, *really* hungry they'd eat one that's hard-boiled."

The cub struggled with the texture at first but ate it all up, using its giant fluffy paw to brush away yellow yolk crumbs from its muzzle. Then it tried

to lick the crumbs that had stuck
to its paw but that meant balancing
awkwardly on three legs. It wobbled, fell
and rolled back on to its feet.

"You're a hilarious little cub!" Fliss
exclaimed. She pulled the lion towards
her. "But I can't keep calling you 'cub'
or 'little lion'. You need a proper name."

The cub looked at her and replied
with a squeaky roar.

"I think it'll have to be one I can
pronounce!" she said. "You need a name
that is worldly and wise, because one
day I just know you're going to grow
up to be a magnificent... Oh!" Fliss
realized she had no idea if the cub was
a boy or girl. She had a quick look. "A
magnificent *lioness*!"

Fliss placed the little lioness in the

grass next to her. It looked so at home here, so much part of the landscape. To give it a normal human name like Lily or Rosie just wouldn't do. A funny name like Bobkin wouldn't do either. She needed a name that belonged in this world.

"How about Serengeti or Africa? No, those names are too big for a small cub... Wait! We're in Tanzania, so how about Tanzy for short? It's pretty and sweet – now isn't that the perfect name for you?"

Tanzy batted her paw clumsily at a fly that kept buzzing around her nose. Fliss let her play while she concentrated on what to do next. Thinking hard, she remembered that north of the Serengeti was the Mara River. It was where some

of the great migrations took place.
Animals crossed over it to look for
cooler temperatures and more food in
the Masai Mara Park on the other side,
in the next-door country of Kenya. The
Mara River was a source of water and
food. In fact, it could be just the place
to find a pride of lions, tired and thirsty
from a fight.

"That's it, Tanzy!" Fliss exclaimed.
"We need to find the river!"

# The Sound of Thunder

Fliss was finding it hard to pack away her lunchbox with Tanzy leaping all over her. The little cub was gaining more and more confidence every minute! She wriggled and climbed, and Fliss had to pick her up and put her back down on the ground.

"I love you, too!" She sighed, happily. "But let me sort out my bag. We can't leave any litter behind."

But then Tanzy wrapped her front

paws around Fliss's arm, weighing it down, and started to nibble on Fliss's thumb.

"Ow! Those little teeth of yours are spikey!"

With her free hand, Fliss grabbed Tanzy's muzzle lightly and Tanzy clawed back, trying to get her teeth into Fliss's wrist. It didn't hurt, it just tickled.

"You're suddenly very playful so I guess you must be feeling better."

Without warning, Tanzy leaped on to her shoulder and the two of them rolled in the grass. Tanzy was getting more excited by the rough-and-tumble action, and Fliss was loving every moment. This could be the only chance she ever got to be a lion cub's playmate.

But play-fighting wasn't something cubs did just for fun – it helped to train them in the skills of hunting and killing. Being away from the pride meant Tanzy could be missing out on important life lessons from her siblings and parents. And if Tanzy didn't learn to be the hunter, then she could end up being the prey. Without her lion skills she'd never survive the Serengeti.

The truth made Fliss focus. She had to deliver the cub to safety and then find a way home. She had no more water and her throat was starting to scratch with thirst. There was no time to lose. Fliss grabbed Tanzy gently by the scruff of her neck, just as a mother lion would do, and put her down on the ground.

"Enough messing around. We have a river to find."

Heaving the bag over her shoulder, Fliss stepped out of the shade of the tree and immediately felt the heat tingle on her skin. Tanzy trotted to her side, ready for the next step in their adventure.

"That's right, Tanzy. I want you to stay by my side every step of the way," Fliss said, smiling down at her companion. "Just as soon as I work out which way to go…"

With no idea where in the Serengeti she was, how would ever find the Mara River?

A group of birds flew overhead – seven or eight of them, all in a straight line. They were brown and white, with huge finger-tipped wings, skinny necks and long thin legs. *They look a bit like herons or cranes*, Fliss thought. *They could be water birds!*

Tanzy had spotted another grasshopper and was about to bound away on a hopeless mission to catch it.

"Oh, no you don't..." Fliss tutted. She steered the cub away gently with her foot. "There's no time to chase grasshoppers. We have to follow the birds!"

Striding through the grasses under the blazing sun, Fliss became uncomfortably hot. Her clothes were sticky and her feet were baking in her shoes. If this had been a family walk or a PE lesson, she would have sat on the ground and refused to move another inch. But she had a promise to keep and that kept her going.

"It ... can't ... be ... far ... now," she puffed. "Look, Tanzy. More water birds and they're flying in the same direction as the first flock. We have to be close!"

Tanzy seemed to understand the encouragement in her voice and meowed.

Heat rippled the air and apart from the chirrup of locusts and grasshoppers, the plains were eerily quiet. There was nothing but the noise of their footsteps scuffing the ground and the occasional whoosh of the breeze through the grasses. Tanzy bounced ahead and Fliss walked steadily on behind, one foot after the other, eyes on the sky to see which way the birds were flying.

A drumming sound interrupted her rhythm.

What was that? It reminded her of horses, like hooves pummelling dry earth. Fliss searched the horizon for a clue but there was nothing out there and it was getting louder. Within seconds, the hoof beats were rumbling like incoming thunder and the vibrations juddered through Fliss's body.

She spun round and there behind her, in a flurry of brown dust, was a stampeding herd. The charging beasts were large and grey. They were approaching so fast that it wasn't long before she could see their bony backs, grizzly beards and sharp horns.

"Wildebeest!" she exclaimed. "Tanzy!"

Fliss scooped Tanzy off the ground. Clutching the cub tight to her chest, she ran to the closest tree. The acacia tree with its umbrella canopy had plenty of branches to climb, if there was time…

The wildebeest were so close now she could see the flare of their nostrils and the way they lowered their horned heads as if they were butting the air in front of them!

"Quick, Tanzy!" She raised the cub as high up the trunk as she could reach. "Climb!"

The cub scrambled to the top but Fliss knew there'd be no time to follow safely. If she slipped and fell she'd be trampled. She flattened herself against the trunk, arms tight against her body. The animals stampeded by, streaming either side of the tree, which was now like an island in a fast-flowing river of wildebeest. The noise was deafening. The hooves sent the dusty earth billowing up in clouds. Fliss closed her eyes tight.

When it was over she sighed with
relief. "Who knew herbivores could be
so dangerous!"

Fliss wiped the dust from her eyes
and looked up. The cub was high up
in the tree, shaking.

"It's OK, you can come down now."

But Tanzy looked paralyzed.

"Hang on, little one!" Fliss began
to climb the cat's cradle of branches,
pulling herself right to the top where
the cub was shivering. She reached out
and Tanzy leaped right into her arms
and hid her face in Fliss's neck.

Comforting the cub, Fliss stopped to
catch her breath and take a look at the
view. The tree wasn't very tall but being
higher up allowed her to see right across
the land. As the disturbed earth settled,
Fliss noticed something ahead – a huge
glittering ribbon, looping and snaking
through the landscape. No more than a
kilometre or two away.

"The Mara River!"

# Journey to the Mara

Fliss stayed a little while longer in the tree, sitting in the fork of two branches, swinging her legs. As the warm wind fluttered her hair she began to laugh. Only moments before she had been tired and frightened, but now she felt more alive than ever. Was it the dry Serengeti air? The view of the great Mara River in the distance? Perhaps it was the thrill of the stampeding wildebeest…

"Why do you think I feel this way, hey?" she asked the cub. Tanzy gave her neck a prickly lick. "Oh, you think it's because of you, do you? You know, Tanzy, I thought I'd go home today without seeing any lions at all. Now look at me, right here in the land of the lions. And I've got a feeling it was you who brought me here."

Was it dust in the cub's eye or did Tanzy actually wink?

"Come on. It's probably time we both went home."

Fliss carefully climbed back down the tree with Tanzy in one arm. After the race of the wildebeest, the plains were calm once again. Fliss marvelled at how everything could be so dramatic one minute and sleepy and serene the next. The sun-bathed landscape was almost hypnotic.

Heat played lots of tricks – it made everything on the horizon look like liquid. She had once read a story about a desert mirage, where the heat took away all the colour of the sand so it looked like water. In the story, the thirsty travellers thought it was an oasis in the distance.

Was that what she was seeing now, over there?

Just up ahead – too close to be the river – the ground was fuzzy and out of focus. It was shimmering. What *was* that? She hadn't spotted it from her position in the tree. It looked like a silvery sheet. It looked like water. *Water...* Fliss felt her throat tighten. There were waterholes in the Serengeti – perhaps one would be fed by a freshwater spring. She licked her dry lips at the thought of cool clean water and began to run towards it.

But the closer she got, the more confused she became. There was still a shimmer, but in it she noticed a nose and two ears. Four tails. Then individual shapes began to emerge from the confusing pattern. Fliss could see now. The animals' stripes meant that from a distance they had no solid outline – they melted together into one large mass. From a distance it was impossible to tell what they were.

"Oh my goodness!" Fliss gasped. "That is the cleverest camouflage I've ever seen!"

The dazzle of zebras parted as Fliss walked right through them, eyes wide in amazement.

They looked like stubby stripey horses – something that could have been conjured up by a wizard. Even their manes were striped! Fliss wished Ella could see this – she was the world's biggest lover of zebras. Or *zee*-bras – she liked to say it the American way for fun. Fliss felt a lump in her throat at the thought of her friend, who would be missing her. But all she had to do to feel better was look at Tanzy and remember her vet's oath.

Fliss and Tanzy continued on towards the Mara River. The closer they got, the more animals they saw emerging from the plains. They walked alongside graceful gazelles and impalas with twisty horns and pretty patterns. Fliss's stomach fluttered with excitement –

she was so close to Africa's incredible wildlife! It also fluttered with fear, because among the Serengeti's native animals were some very dangerous species. If other animals were coming to the river, then the dangerous ones would be coming, too.

Keeping an eye out for sudden stampedes, Fliss kept going. The sun beating down on her head made her sleepy. Her dry eyes blinked against the hot air and dust. But just a few more minutes and they'd be there. Then they would find the pride and she could concentrate on getting home.

The Mara River wasn't as Fliss had imagined. The pictures at the school centre had shown raging torrents and animals struggling to get through the

fast waters, but over the summer there
hadn't been much rain in the Serengeti
and the river was low. Large rocks
created stepping stones across it and
areas of the riverbed stuck out of the
shallow waters, making sandy islands
for birds and tired beasts to sit on.
Fliss had no idea that so many different
animals – some of which she was sure
would quite like to eat each other –
could rest happily side-by-side.

"Shall we take a closer look, Tanzy? Do
you think they'll make room for us?"

There were antelope, wildebeest and
zebras drinking. Hippos basked on rocks
or bobbed around in small pools, some
with birds standing on their heads. Fliss
looked left and right. There were birds
and beasts as far as the eye could see.

But where were the lions?

Fliss turned in circles, hoping to see a glimpse of golden fur among the brown and grey, but there was no sign of them.

"Oh, Tanzy, they're not here," Fliss said. She tried to stay calm in case the cub got upset. But her heart was racing. She was so certain they'd be here. They might have crossed the waters, Fliss supposed, although on the other side she could see ... elephants! Wow!

The peaceful herd of beautiful creatures stood at the water's edge, their trunks swaying and their ears flapping gently. They were happy.

And then, suddenly, they weren't.

Without warning, a large elephant broke into a run. It headed away from the river and into the foliage behind. Its ear-splitting trumpet blasted the air like a danger siren, and then the other members of its herd began running, too. They were fast on their feet, trampling the bushes and small trees to get away.

Other animals at the edge of the river began to panic, too. Impalas backed away from the water, stepping on top of one another as they fled. Fliss's heart started beating so fast she could feel it against her ribs. She couldn't see

anything but she sensed trouble. The
air seemed to fizz with electricity. Tanzy
picked up on it, too. Her eyes were wide
and scared.

"What's going on, Tanzy?"

Fliss searched for a sign but it didn't
look as if there had been a crocodile
attack or any hippos getting feisty.
In fact, all the animals in the river
were calm. It was the animals on
land that were shrieking and bucking
and jumping in all directions. The
commotion got louder and louder.

Tanzy knew what was happening,
though. The cub was looking to the
right, roaring over and over at an
invisible enemy. Fliss followed her line
of sight.

Cheetahs.

# Danger, Everywhere

Fliss and Tanzy stood absolutely still. Further around the bend of the river – less than a football pitch away – three cheetahs were making their way through a clump of trees. They walked slowly and carefully, spread out like a sports team. Fliss guessed it was how they attacked – from all angles.

With every step they took, a wave of animals scattered and soon there were beasts running everywhere, herds colliding in panic. If Fliss and Tanzy didn't move now they'd either be trampled or on a cheetah's menu!

"Let's go!" Fliss grabbed Tanzy, who was still roaring bravely, and pulled her up into her arms. Which way should they go? With wildebeest, deer, zebras and cheetahs running wild, there was nowhere safe. She spotted a stack of rocks to her left, a few metres back from the river. Cheetahs would be able to climb them easily but they had their sights set on the water, where a group of young gazelles was caught in the muddy shallows. Fliss scrambled up one of the rocks, clutching Tanzy tightly. The cub's paws and head rested over one of Fliss's shoulders as she continued to roar at the cheetahs.

"Don't be scared," Fliss said, although at that moment she was as scared as she'd ever been. She turned to look at the scene by the river.

The cheetahs were still heading for the water, closing in like a net – walking slowly, occasionally lying low,

getting closer and closer. And then –
the sprint! The cheetahs burst into a
run so fast it took Fliss's breath away.
The gazelles, croaking and bleating
in panic, struggled urgently in the
mud. Most of them broke free and
scampered away, zigzagging across the
land to confuse the cats, but one was
stuck, its thin legs wedged into the
riverbed.

Fliss prayed it would get away in time,
but if it did then the cheetahs would
go hungry. *This is nature*, she reminded
herself. *Beautiful but cruel.* She turned
away. She didn't want to see what
would happen next. She buried her face
in Tanzy's fur and kept it there until
Tanzy, no longer roaring, gave her a
nudge under her chin.

Fliss
looked up.
The little
gazelle was
covered
in mud but
bounding away
across the plains while
the cheetahs slunk back into the trees.

"That was one lucky gazelle," she said.
Tanzy gave her a big prickly lick right
across her cheek. "Now it's time we made
sure you have a happy ending, too!"

But she didn't have a clue what to
do or where to go. She'd been so sure
the lions would be at the river that
she hadn't planned what to do if they
weren't there.

She looked out over the plains. The

Serengeti was so big and wild. She and
Tanzy were just two small animals,
and suddenly Fliss didn't feel so brave
about her mission. On top of that, she
had started to feel shaky. Her stomach
groaned with hunger and her throat was
raw and dry. Her head was dizzy with
heat. She sat down quickly before her
legs gave way.

She looked at Tanzy in her lap. The
cub's eyes were half closed.

"Do you need a nap, little one?" Fliss
said, gently stroking Tanzy's head. "Or
are you feeling weak, like me?"

Tanzy tried to roar but nothing came
out – not even a squeak – and Fliss
felt hot tears in her eyes. This cub
needed food and lioness's milk soon or
she might not survive. Jonty's words

echoed in her mind. *Being a vet is a tough job ... but it looks to me like you have determination...*

If Jonty could see her now, perhaps he wouldn't think she had what it took. But being a vet was all she wanted to do, so she had to find strength and determination from somewhere.

"I made a vet's oath and I can't break it," she said aloud.

Fliss closed her eyes, breathed in deeply and gathered her thoughts. Before she decided where to go next, Tanzy needed attention.

"Lions get most of their moisture from food. But you've only had some dry chicken and a tiny egg. That's where we'll start – we'll get you a drink of water."

Cradling Tanzy, Fliss headed away

from the remaining wildebeest and along the riverbank. When she found an area where there were no animals that could run, jump or cause a commotion, she approached the water's edge. Tanzy started to wriggle in her arms, as if she could smell the water.

"Wait, Tanzy," Fliss said. "I'm not going to put you down yet. Not until I'm absolutely sure it's safe. I've read about crocodiles and I don't think I'd like to meet one!"

Fliss threw a few big sticks into the shallows in front of her. If there was a crocodile there it would leap or wriggle with surprise – or attack. But after each splash, the water was still.

Holding on tight to Tanzy's body, she let the cub lap.

The sun-sparkles danced on the river
and Fliss was tempted to dip her hand
into it and cup some of the water to
her mouth. But this wasn't a freshwater
spring and Fliss knew that her stomach
would not be used to the bacteria in the
water. It could make her sick. And what
use was a sick vet?

She pushed her thirst from her mind
and instead concentrated on staying
alert and being ready to run, just like an
animal of the Serengeti.

After drinking, Tanzy broke away
from her grip and tried to hop across
some rocks by the bank to investigate
the birds perched there.

"No you don't, little one." Fliss was
so parched her voice was just a whisper
now. "There'll be plenty of time to
play when you find your brothers and
sisters."

But where were Tanzy's siblings?
Where were her mother and father?
Where would she and Tanzy even start
to look for them?

She took out the postcard – it was the
only clue she had.

# Serengeti Daze

The lioness in the picture was now
sitting on her hind legs, her head high.
Other lionesses were standing next
to her, peering in different directions.
They were on the lookout.

"Where are you?" Fliss whispered,
stroking the picture. She felt her
fingertips tingle. Then she recognized
a patch of flattened grass behind the
pride, a little way in the distance.

"Tanzy, they're waiting for you," Fliss

said, brightening. "They haven't given up and moved on at all. Of course! If it was me, I'd be staying close to where I lost you… So that's where we should go – back to where it all started." That place with the claw marks and tufts of lion mane – that was where the cub had got lost. The pride would have found a safe place to rest or hide but they wouldn't have moved too far away from where the cub went missing.

"No one could abandon you, Tanzy," Fliss said to the now lively cub.

Fliss looked again at the Mara River and the lush green fields and trees on the other side of it. It felt wrong to be walking away from it but she was certain it was the right thing to do.

She turned round and, with Tanzy at

her side, began walking against the tide of deer heading for the river. The deer leaped aside when they got near but then regrouped and continued their journey. In this heat, any sensible animal would be heading for water. Once again, Fliss had to push away thoughts of fresh water and how freely it flowed back home.

Home. She suddenly missed it like crazy. She missed the cool air. She missed crisp apples and fruit juice and sliced-up cucumbers. She missed her soft bed. Any bed. She was so tired she could sleep anywhere – up an acacia tree, in the long grasses, on a Serengeti rock… She just needed sleep.

Tanzy brushed against her ankle and gave a little squeak, looking up at her and blinking against the bright sunlight.

Fliss jolted awake. She'd been walking with her eyes closed in a daze! She woke herself up by shaking out her arms and legs.

"I'm going to be strong for you, Tanzy," Fliss said, holding back the tears. "I made a promise as a vet and as your friend."

Fliss knew that she would never break her promise. She just hoped that the wild Serengeti wouldn't break her first.

Fliss tripped and stumbled across the land. She kept her eyes on Tanzy as she repeated her vet's oath, over and over. It kept her going when she thought she might melt in the heat. But although she forced her brain to stay focused, Fliss's legs were tiring. Her footsteps slowed down until eventually she came to a stop.

She couldn't take another step. Tanzy circled her and pawed at her legs with worry.

"I'm OK, Tanzy, I'm OK," Fliss whispered, sitting down. "But we've been walking a very long time. Give me minute to rest and we'll be on our way again."

Even as she was saying the words, Fliss felt her body sinking lower into the grass. She fell asleep before her head even touched the ground.

Fliss felt a tickling on her cheek. What was that? In her sleepy daze she thought it was Tanzy's whiskers and smiled, but as the tickling spread across her face and down her neck, she woke in alarm.

Ants! Argh! Fliss leaped up, brushing the little brown ants from her face and neck. Even after she'd got rid of them, she carried on wriggling and itching as if they were still crawling on her. What a horrible feeling! Her head wasn't any better either – it hurt from sleeping out in the sun. But that wasn't the worst thing.

Tanzy was nowhere to be seen.

Fliss looked out across the plains. The

sun was low and the blue sky had turned pinky-orange like a ripe apricot. How long had she been asleep? How long had the cub been missing?

"Tanzy!" she called. Her thirsty voice was so cracked it didn't carry far. "Tanzy, where are you?"

Fliss sat back down and held her head in her hands. Everything hurt. Her head ached and her heart was sore... Tanzy ... little Tanzy...

She couldn't give up. If she did she'd be no good to anyone. Fliss squeezed her eyes shut and took several deep breaths to calm herself down.

Another annoying ant found its way on to her face and she brushed it away with the back of her hand. It came back again, this time with friends. She felt their footsteps tickle her chin. She wanted to scream. She opened her eyes, ready to leap up and pat herself down…

*Oh!* Tanzy nuzzled her chin. It wasn't ants – it *was* whiskers this time!

"Thank goodness!" Fliss said. She still felt like crying but this time with relief. The cub was safe. "Come for a cuddle. I could really do with one."

But Tanzy had different ideas. She ran ahead into the grasses, then stopped and looked back. Then she did the same again and again.

"Do you want me to follow you?"

Fliss rose to her feet, wobbling like a tree in a heat haze. She didn't feel like she had the energy to start walking again just yet but the lions might be close. Concentrating on putting one foot in front of the other, she followed Tanzy. Fliss didn't notice the strange-looking creature ahead of them until... *Snoo-ink*! The noise was like a long pig's oink. But it wasn't a pig.

The weird animal looked like an enormous ferret with a stripe of grey fur on top and black fur underneath, and it was leaning over a large broken tree branch. Fliss narrowed her eyes and tried to focus. As she stepped closer it turned and bared its teeth, before running away.

"What was that, Tanzy?" Fliss said. But the cub knew exactly what it was. She had already run to where the creature had been and was licking at the branch, where a couple of dozy bees were circling. Dark amber oozed liquid from a hole in the top.

So hungry her tummy was twisting in knots, Fliss decided that if it was good enough for a lion, it was good enough for her... She scooped some of the sticky liquid on to her finger and tasted it. Such sweetness! Fliss's face lit up.

"Wonderful raw honey! That must have been a honey badger. I remember seeing it in my animal encyclopedia. We're lucky, Tanzy. Honey badgers can be vicious. Did you see those teeth?"

Tanzy wasn't listening. She was

feasting, making funny, snarly faces
as she tried to lick the honey sticking
to her gums. Fliss scooped out more
honey for herself. She licked her finger
with a satisfying slurp. She might have
missed out on ice cream back at the
zoo, but this was the sweetest thing
she'd ever tasted.

"Clever bees for making the honey. Clever badger for finding the hive. And clever Tanzy, for sniffing it out. You're the best!"

The natural sugars in the honey filled her with energy. She felt amazing. This was power food and it was delicious. Tanzy thought so, too, although the cub was now struggling with her sticky whiskers and was trying to reach her tongue all around her face.

"Come on, funny thing!" Fliss laughed. "Let's leave some honey for the poor badger. I've got a feeling he was too weak to fight and needs that honey to build his strength. Besides, it's time we got you some proper lion food!"

# A Laughing Matter

Her throat was still dry but the honey had given her energy. There would be no more sleeping now. Not until Tanzy was safely home. Fliss felt determined. Now there was nothing but a stretch of grassland between them and the pride. She and Tanzy set off once again, this time with a skip and a made-up song.

*Full of love and honey inside, we'll keep going until we find Tanzy's pride!*

In Fliss's rush of happiness, she forgot

about the dangers around them. Then
a sudden screech stopped her in her
tracks. A chill went down her spine. She
didn't know what it was but it could
only be an animal of some sort and
there was nowhere to hide. She tucked
Tanzy under her arm and crouched
in the long grasses. She gathered her
Serengeti wits and listened closely.

There it was again… The horrible
noise was made up of ten, maybe
twenty different voices. Peeking over the
grass, she saw group of fluffy, spotted
animals running at full speed. Hyenas!
Everyone knew about hyenas. They
were pack hunters and they were known
to attack humans.

The hyenas were running as fast as
their legs could carry them but Fliss

couldn't see what they were chasing. There was nothing in front of them.

Eventually they slowed and stopped. Some sat on the ground exhausted and others paced around them. Their screeches turned to laughter. The cackling sound made Fliss want to giggle. But they weren't laughing – they were bickering among themselves. Fliss turned away. She didn't want to see any more fights and besides, she was busy trying to work something out.

If those hyenas hadn't been chasing something, then maybe they were running *from* something ... and there was only one beast that scared hyenas that much.

Lions!

Scanning the land, Fliss couldn't see any but that didn't mean they weren't there. Her heart began to pound – she was excited for Tanzy but also frightened. In her short experience in the Serengeti, she knew animals could appear out of nowhere – running across the plains, hunting or being hunted... She suddenly felt very exposed. Standing in the middle of the plains with no speed in her legs and a small cub to care for meant she was as vulnerable as a gazelle and not even half as fast. Fliss thought of all the animals she'd seen that day. If you're not tough like a wildebeest, if you can't run fast like a deer, if you can't attack like a cheetah … what do you do? Then Fliss remembered the zebras. Camouflage!

She grabbed handfuls of the golden grasses and stuffed them into her clothing and hair. She now looked like a scarecrow and she itched like crazy all over, but if she stayed low she'd be well hidden.

There was an outcrop in the distance close to the fighting spot. She could rest and think about her next move there. If she hadn't had all that honey she would never have made it and Fliss thanked Tanzy once more with a good scratch behind the ears. Then they were on their way, running low and fast through the grasses towards the outcrop.

At the base of it, they sat down in the shade of a tree and caught their breath. Grasshoppers popped out of the grasses all around them but Tanzy didn't seem interested. She looked at Fliss and let out a squeaky roar.

"Are you trying to tell me something?" Fliss said, reaching for her. But Tanzy backed away and roared again. Fliss jumped to her feet. "What is it, Tanzy?"

Then she heard it for herself. A low, grumble that echoed against the giant stones. Tanzy went perfectly still. Fliss gasped.

"It's your pride. They're calling for you."

Fliss bubbled with excitement. This was what they'd been waiting for. She wanted to gather Tanzy in her arms and deliver her to the lioness and say "I looked after her for you", but she knew that wouldn't be possible.

"Your mother desperately wants to see you, Tanzy," she said, crouching down to look into the cub's eyes. "But I don't think she'll want to see me. She might think I took you away from her."

Tanzy snapped at a passing fly, revealing her tiny razor-sharp teeth.

"Or she might be hungry," Fliss added with a gulp.

The lioness's call came again. Tanzy walked a few paces ahead before turning back to look at Fliss.

"Yes, Tanzy, it's time to go," Fliss said, putting on a brave smile. Tanzy stared at her and didn't move. "Come on, then, I'll walk some of the way with you."

Together they walked around the base of the outcrop. The lions must have sensed Tanzy was near because their roars weren't low and long and sad – they burst high and loud and full of

hope. Fliss was frightened now. This
wasn't Pride of Place. There was no
fence between her and Africa's most
famous killer cats. It would be silly to
go any further.

She crouched down, took Tanzy's face
in her hands and looked into those sweet
brown eyes for the final time.

"You'll have to do the last bit on your own."

Tanzy leaped into her arms.

"Oh! I am going to miss you too," Fliss sniffed. "But this is how it has to be. This is your world, not mine."

Tanzy pressed her soft triangle nose against Fliss's cheek. Then Fliss let go and gave her a nudge.

"Go," she whispered. "I promised to look after you and I did. Now I promise never to forget you and I won't. I could never forget you, Tanzy."

## 11

## Pride of Place

Fliss began to climb the rocks as fast as she could. She didn't stop until she reached the top, where she found a scrubby bush to hide behind. She looked down at the grassland below where Tanzy was moving unsteadily towards the sound of her mother's voice. Fliss ran to the other side of the outcrop's large, flat top to look down. She gasped. The whole pride was there – two lions, five lionesses and seven

little cubs. They were sitting in the
shade. All but one.

The lioness had started running. Even
from way up in the air, Fliss could tell
by the bounce in her legs it was a very
happy mother. She stopped and roared
again – a deep, thick reverberating
sound. Very soon she would be reunited
with her cub.

Fliss wanted to cheer, whoop and clap, but she had to be silent. She was in the presence of powerful animals. She clamped her hand over her mouth to stop her excited squeals from escaping.

Then there was a roar like she'd never heard before. It was roar of triumph and an announcement – the cub has returned!

All the lions got to their feet as the lost lion came into view. Then – the joy! Tanzy's mother circled her, sniffing and nuzzling. They rubbed cheeks. They roared in short, happy bursts. The other lionesses began running, too, their long tails dancing behind them. Soon Tanzy was engulfed in the love and relief of her mother and aunts, and her brothers and sisters were now springing towards the huddle as fast as their little legs could carry them.

When Tanzy emerged from between
the legs of the adult lions, the cubs
rolled together on
the ground in
one big, fluffy
bundle. The
largest male
lion roared.
Then they got
up and shook the
Serengeti dust from
their coats. It was time to move on. The
two males led the way and the females
ushered the naughty cubs, making sure
every member of the pride was there.

Fliss felt her heart thump as the pride
started to move away from their resting
place, padding deeper into the colour-

changing scenery of the Serengeti.
The yellow sun had melted into a soft
orange and hung low in the sky, turning
the grasses a rosy gold. The acacia and
baobab trees turned to dark silhouettes
with long shadows.

Fliss watched as the lions' shadows
followed in a row behind them. The
smallest one at the back belonged to
Tanzy, who now looked tiny in the
distance.

"Bye bye, Tanzy," Fliss whispered,
her eyes welling with tears. The cub
suddenly stopped and looked back up at
her. Fliss waved and laughed.

But the lioness wasn't going to lose
her cub again – she gave her a hefty bat
in the right direction with her paw and
Tanzy skidded ahead.

Fliss stayed on the rock a while longer, enjoying the cooling breeze and watching the sun go down. It oozed like lava and sizzled on the horizon, and the first star of the night sat high in the peach-and-purple sky like a diamond. With Tanzy safe, Fliss had time to appreciate the magic and beauty of the Serengeti. It was wide and wild. It was totally wonderful.

But it wasn't home.

She pulled out her postcard. The light was fading but the pictures were still clear. The image of the pride had changed. It wasn't lying down but walking, a group of lions, big and small, all facing the same direction. Fliss held her breath and crossed her fingers. It was time to check up on her little lost cub. Was her job done? Could she go home? She tilted the card.

A lion cub stood on its own, its pride in the distance. Its head was cocked to one side and its eyes danced with curiosity. It looked strong and full of health.

"Go, Tanzy!" Fliss laughed. "Hurry and don't stop to play with any grasshoppers on the way!"

She closed her eyes and kissed the picture of her rescued little lion as the cooling breeze brushed across her face.

# 12

# A Special Gift

"Fliss! Come on!"

*What?* Fliss's eyes sprang open. She
turned in circles. No dust, no heat, no
sunset. She was back!

"When did it g-g-get so cold?" she
stammered, her teeth chattering as she
joined Ella who was waiting further
along the walkway.

"It's not cold. And what's this?" Ella
began to pick strands of grass from Fliss's
hair. "Are you turning into a farmer?"

"I don't know," Fliss said. "I – what – what's going on?"

Ella shook her head. "Oh no!"

Jonty appeared. "What the matter here?"

"Fliss has been brainwashed. I think it's those monkeys over there. They look mean."

Jonty laughed. "Enough monkey business – I promised I'd have you back in ten minutes."

Ella wagged her finger at the monkeys. "You leave my friend alone."

While Ella was telling off the monkeys, Fliss tried to pull herself together. She had walked for hours in the Serengeti but not a minute had passed back home. Even so, her skin had grown used to the African sun

and she was now freezing. She rubbed
her arms to get warm.

"Cold?" Jonty asked. "Imagine how the lions feel – living here in a cold climate when they should be in the Serengeti."

"Hmmm," Fliss said, nodding. Although she didn't have to imagine.

Back at the gift shop, Mrs Mullins, Mr Pincent and the assistant teachers had lined the school children up in a row, ready to board the coach.

"There they are!" shouted a girl called Samira.

"We thought you'd been eaten by a lion," said Milos.

Sarah shook her head. "I bet they didn't see any lions at all."

Ella nudged Fliss and gave her a

big wink. "We did, actually," she said confidently. "We saw loads of lions. They were great, weren't they, Fliss?"

"Yep," Fliss nodded.

"Really?" Sarah's jaw dropped open.

"How many male lions were there again, Fliss?"

"Two."

"That's right. Two. And there were three lionesses."

"Five," Fliss corrected.

"Oh yeah, five. And loads of cubs."

"Eight in total," Fliss said, and she couldn't stop a wide smile spreading across her face.

As they left the shop, she grabbed some of the free leaflets, including *African Animals*, which came with a map of the Serengeti on the back.

When she was seated on the coach, she began to mark out where she had been on the page. She drew in umbrella trees and stampeding herds, zebra dazzles, attacking cheetahs and loping giraffes. Next she filled the blue band of the Mara River with hippo heads and penned a honey badger and some hyenas. Then she carefully sketched a pride of lions next to a stack of rocks. Looking down on them from the top, she drew herself.

"What's that – a monkey?"

Ella had grown bored of playing plastic-spider pranks and Dan had pinched her cuddly snake.

"No, that's me."

"You? You wouldn't survive a day in the Spaghetti."

"Do you mean Serengeti?" Fliss said.

Ella started shrieking with laughter and Fliss laughed along with her. She was the funniest person in the world.

"Shame you didn't get a proper gift," Ella said, pointing at Fliss's postcard.

Fliss smiled. *But I did. I got to rescue a very special lion. Isn't that right?* she said to herself as she tilted the card.

And Tanzy, head to one side, winked back.

Rachel Delahaye was born in Australia but has lived in the UK since she was six years old. She studied linguistics and worked as a magazine writer and editor before becoming a children's author. She loves words and animals; when she can combine the two, she is very happy indeed! At home, Rachel loves to read, write and watch wildlife documentaries. Outside, she loves to go walking in woodland. She also follows news about animal rights and the environment and hopes that one day the world will be a better home for all species, not just humans!

Rachel has two lively children and a dog called Rocket, and lives in the beautiful city of Bath.

It was his idea to take us all camping – including my little brother, Cheese (he's the one with the famous bottom).

But it was my little sister, Tomato, who started all the trouble – with a carrot called Cecily Sprout . . .

**Jeremy Strong** once worked in a bakery, putting the jam into three thousand doughnuts every night. Now he puts the jam in stories instead, which he finds much more exciting. At the age of three, he fell out of a first-floor bedroom window and landed on his head. His mother says that this damaged him for the rest of his life and refuses to take any responsibility. He loves writing stories because he says it is 'the only time you alone have complete control and can make anything happen'. His ambition is to make you laugh (or at least snuffle). Jeremy Strong lives near Bath with three cats and a flying cow.

This is the sixth book Jeremy Strong has written about Nicholas and his family.

The first five books, in reading order, are:

**MY DAD'S GOT AN ALLIGATOR!**
**MY GRANNY'S GREAT ESCAPE**
**MY MUM'S GOING TO EXPLODE!**
**MY BROTHER'S FAMOUS BOTTOM**
**MY BROTHER'S FAMOUS BOTTOM GETS PINCHED**

Are you feeling silly enough to read more?

**THE HUNDRED-MILE-AN-HOUR DOG**
**RETURN OF THE HUNDRED-MILE-AN-HOUR DOG**
**WANTED! THE HUNDRED-MILE-AN-HOUR DOG**
**LOST! THE HUNDRED-MILE-AN-HOUR DOG**